MOTHER GOOSE
NURSERY RHYMES

Making Friends

with

MOTHER GOOSE

Compiled by Stephanie Hedlund
Illustrated by Jeremy Tugeau

visit us at www.abdopublishing.com

Published by Magic Wagon, a division of the ABDO Group, 8000 West 78th Street, Edina, Minnesota 55439. Copyright © 2011 by Abdo Consulting Group, Inc. International copyrights reserved in all countries. All rights reserved. No part of this book may be reproduced in any form without written permission from the publisher.

Looking Glass Library™ is a trademark and logo of Magic Wagon.

Printed in the United States of America, North Mankato, Minnesota.
102010
012011
This book contains at least 10% recycled materials.

Compiled by Stephanie Hedlund
Illustrations by Jeremy Tugeau
Edited by Rochelle Baltzer
Cover and interior layout and design by Abbey Fitzgerald

Library of Congress Cataloging-in-Publication Data

Making friends with Mother Goose / compiled by Stephanie Hedlund ; illustrated by Jeremy Tugeau.
    v. cm. -- (Mother Goose nursery rhymes)
   Contents: Nursery rhymes about people -- She sells sea shells -- Georgie Porgie -- Humpty Dumpty -- Little Miss Muffet -- Jack be nimble -- Mary, Mary quite contrary -- Little Bo-Peep -- Yankee Doodle -- Peter, Peter, pumpkin eater -- Jack and Jill -- There was an old woman -- Jack Sprat -- Peter Piper.
   ISBN 978-1-61641-145-9
  1. Nursery rhymes. 2. Children's poetry. [1. Nursery rhymes.] I. Hedlund, Stephanie F., 1977- II. Tugeau, Jeremy, ill. III. Mother Goose.
   PZ8.3.M288 2011
   398.8 [E]--dc22
                        2010024697

Contents

Nursery Rhymes
About People

Since early days, people have created rhymes to teach and entertain children. Since they were often said in a nursery, they became known as nursery rhymes. In the 1700s, these nursery rhymes were collected and published to share with parents and other adults.

Some of these collections were named after Mother Goose. Mother Goose didn't actually exist, but there are many stories about who she could be. Her rhymes were so popular, people began using *Mother Goose* rhymes to refer to most nursery rhymes.

Since the 1600s, nursery rhymes have come from many sources. The meanings of the rhymes have been lost, but they are an important form of folk language. Nursery rhymes about people are usually fun tongue twisters or introduce you to interesting characters.

She Sells Sea Shells

She sells sea shells on the seashore;

The shells that she sells are sea shells I'm sure.

So if she sells sea shells on the seashore,

I'm sure that the shells are seashore shells.

Georgie Porgie

Georgie Porgie, pudding and pie,

Kissed the girls and made them cry;

When the boys came out to play,

Georgie Porgie ran away.

Humpty Dumpty

Humpty Dumpty sat on a wall,
Humpty Dumpty had a great fall;
All the king's horses and all the king's men
Couldn't put Humpty together again.

Little Miss Muffet

Little Miss Muffet
Sat on a tuffet
Eating her curds and whey;
There came a big spider,
Who sat down beside her
And frightened Miss Muffet away.

Jack Be Nimble

Jack be nimble,
Jack be quick,
Jack jump over
The candlestick.

15

Mary, Mary, Quite Contrary

Mary, Mary, quite contrary,

How does your garden grow?

With silver bells and cockleshells,

And pretty maids all in a row.

Little Bo-Peep

Little Bo-Peep has lost her sheep
And doesn't know where to find them;
Leave them alone, and they'll come home,
Bringing their tails behind them.

Little Bo-Peep fell fast asleep
And dreamed she heard them bleating;
But when she awoke, she found it a joke,
For they were still a fleeting.

Then up she took her little crook,
Determined for to find them;
She found them indeed, but it made her heart bleed,
For they'd left their tails behind them.

It happened one day, as Bo-Peep did stray
Into a meadow hard by;
There she espied their tails side by side,
All hung on a tree to dry.

She heaved a sigh, and wiped her eye,
And over the hillocks went rambling,
And tried what she could, as a shepherdess should,
To tack again each to its lambkin.

Yankee Doodle

Yankee Doodle went to town,
Riding on a pony.
Stuck a feather in his hat
And called it macaroni.

Yankee Doodle keep it up,
Yankee Doodle dandy.
Mind the music and the step
And with the girls be handy.

Peter, Peter, Pumpkin Eater

Peter, Peter, pumpkin eater,

Had a wife and couldn't keep her;

He put her in a pumpkin shell

And there he kept her very well.

Jack and Jill

Jack and Jill went up the hill
To fetch a pail of water;
Jack fell down and broke his crown,
And Jill came tumbling after.

Up Jack got, and home did trot
As fast as he could caper,
To old Dame Dob, who patched his nob
With vinegar and brown paper.

When Jill came in, how she did grin
To see Jack's paper plaster;
Dame Dob, vexed, did whip her
For causing Jack's disaster.

There Was an Old Woman

There was an old woman who lived in a shoe,

She had so many children,

She didn't know what to do,

She gave them some broth without any bread;

She whipped them all soundly and put them to bed.

Jack Sprat

Jack Sprat could eat no fat,

His wife could eat no lean,

And so between them both, you see,

They licked the platter clean.

Peter Piper

Peter Piper picked a peck of pickled peppers;

A peck of pickled peppers Peter Piper picked;

If Peter Piper picked a peck of pickled peppers,

Where's the peck of pickled peppers Peter Piper picked?

Glossary

bleat – the natural cry of a sheep or goat.
caper – to leap or prance playfully.
cockleshells – the hard case of a cockle.
contrary – being in conflict with others.
crook – a shepherd's staff.
curds – the thick, creamy part of thickened milk.
dame – the woman who is head of a house.
espied – to catch sight of something or someone.
fleeting – moving away or vanishing.
hillock – a small hill.
lambkin – a small or young lamb.
nimble – a quick or light motion.
nob – head.
peck – a large number of an item.
tuffet – a low seat.
vexed – annoyed.
whey – the watery part of milk that is separated from curds when making cheese.

Web Sites

To learn more about nursery rhymes, visit ABDO Group online at **www.abdopublishing.com**. Web sites about nursery rhymes are featured on our Book Links page. These links are routinely monitored and updated to provide the most current information available.